WORLDWIDE ADVENTURES 2

The Great Egyptian
Grave Robbery

FLAT STANLEY's
WORLDWIDE ADVENTURES BOOK No. 2

The Great Egyptian
Grave Robbery

CREATED BY **Jeff Brown**
WRITTEN BY **Sara Pennypacker**
PICTURES BY **Macky Pamintuan**

SCHOLASTIC INC.
New York Toronto London Auckland
Sydney Mexico City New Delhi Hong Kong

ISBN: 978-0-545-20684-6

Text copyright © 2009 by the Trust u/w/o Richard C. Brown a/k/a Jeff Brown f/b/o Duncan Brown. Illustrations by Macky Pamintuan, copyright © 2009 by HarperCollins Publishers. All rights reserved. Published by Scholastic Inc., 557 Broadway, New York, NY 10012, by arrangement with HarperCollins Children's Books, a division of HarperCollins Publishers. SCHOLASTIC and associated logos are trademarks and/or registered trademarks of Scholastic Inc.

20 19 18   14 15/0

Printed in the U.S.A.   40

First Scholastic printing, January 2010

Typography by Jennifer Heuer

CONTENTS

A Letter for Stanley

George Lambchop was sitting at the
kitchen table, going through the mail
as his wife cooked breakfast. "Look
at these beauties, Harriet!" he called,
holding up a letter with many exotic
stamps in the corner. "From Egypt!"

Ever since their eldest son, Stanley,
had been flattened by a bulletin board

and could now travel by mail, the Lambchop family had become keenly interested in stamps.

"In a minute, dear," Mrs. Lambchop said. "I'm just at the difficult part of flipping this French toast. A letter from Egypt, you say! Why don't you open it and read it to me."

Mr. Lambchop began to do just that, but then he caught himself. "That was a close one!" he cried. "It's a federal offense to open mail that's addressed to someone else. This letter is for Stanley!"

Just then, both Lambchop boys appeared in the doorway, drawn by the delicious aroma of French toast and bacon.

"Stanley, son, letter for you here. Looks important."

"What about me?" Stanley's younger brother, Arthur, asked. "Any mail for me today?"

"Not today, sorry," Mr. Lambchop replied. "But, Stanley, why don't you open yours and read it to us over breakfast."

"*After* breakfast," Mrs. Lambchop said firmly. "*And* hand washing. You know how maple syrup gets all over everything."

The boys finished their breakfast

and washed up. Then Stanley opened his letter.

"If you are the world-famous flattened boy of America," he read out loud, "and if you are less than three inches thick, you must come to Egypt at once. We are beginning an archaeological project and are in urgent need of someone of your dimensions."

"I don't know about *world-famous*," Arthur grumbled—a bit enviously, it must be said.

"Maybe they've got the wrong person."

"But I *am* only half an inch thick." Stanley sighed. "So that's me, all right."

"*I*," Mrs. Lambchop corrected her son. "That is *I*."

"It's signed Sir Abu Shenti Hawara the fourth," Stanley said, "and look: He's taken care of my travel arrangements." Stanley held up a very large envelope covered with stamps.

George Lambchop took the letter and read it over. "No mention of Stanley's *family* going with him," he said, frowning. "I don't know . . ."

"Well, an archaeological project . . .

it's not as if it's something dangerous. And travel *is* broadening, George . . . ," Mrs. Lambchop mused. "Oh, Stanley, darling . . . I didn't mean it that way! What I meant was, it rounds out one's education . . . oh my, that didn't come out quite right either!"

"Well, your mother and I have always encouraged you boys to lend a helping hand when needed," Mr. Lambchop said. "I suppose that goes even if it's needed halfway around the world."

"We'd better take you to the post office at once, Stanley," Mrs. Lambchop said. "I will pack the leftover French toast and bacon for you to eat on the way. No maple syrup, of course. It wouldn't do to arrive all sticky!"

"Something to drink?" Stanley asked.

"I think not, dear," his mother told him. "Egypt is quite a distance, and I'm afraid you won't be near a bathroom for some time. Which reminds me . . ." And she went off to pack a toothbrush and washcloth for her son's trip.

Stanley noticed that Arthur seemed glum. He knew Arthur sometimes found it difficult being the only round brother in a family. "Would you like me to bring back something from Egypt for you?" he asked.

"Hmmmph," Arthur replied. "If

you're going to Egypt, you should bring me back a mummy."

"I don't believe they offer those as souvenirs. And besides, it wouldn't fit in the envelope with Stanley!" chuckled the boys' father. Mr. Lambchop was known for his sharp sense of humor. "How about a nice postcard?" Mr. Lambchop was known for being a practical thinker, too.

Arthur folded his hands across his chest. "A mummy or nothing."

Stanley was very sorry to see his brother looking so grumpy as he slid himself into the envelope.

Amisi

The journey was very long—much, much longer than his trip to California. At last he arrived, and just in time. "Let me out, please," he cried. "I'm broiling in here!"

"Sorry," came an official-sounding voice. "An envelope can be opened only by the person to whom it is addressed. Whoever you are, you will have to wait until you are delivered tomorrow."

Just then, Stanley heard another voice . . . the voice of a young girl.

"That package is *flat*!" the voice said. Then it came closer. "You in there!" it demanded. "Do you happen to be . . . Stanley Lambchop of America?"

"I am!" Stanley cried in astonishment. "But how do you know . . . ?"

"Open this package," the girl said to the postmaster. "I will take full responsibility. I will hand deliver the contents to its destination . . . it's an antiquities bazaar, right across from my father's office."

As soon as the flap was opened, Stanley burst out from the envelope to greet his liberator.

"Hello! My name is Amisi," the girl
said, smiling. "I am very

pleased to meet you, Stanley."

"But how do you know who I am?"

Amisi smiled even more broadly. "My father is the curator of the National Historical Museum. He is also a member of the Museum Curators' Worldwide Pen Pal Club. His pen pal is—"

"Mr. O. Jay Dart!" Stanley guessed, delighted. Mr. O. Jay Dart was Stanley's upstairs neighbor. He was also the curator of the Famous Museum, and not long ago Stanley had helped him out with a certain predicament involving sneak thieves.

"Right!" Amisi agreed. "When Mr. Dart wrote to him about what you did, my father couldn't stop talking about you. He said he wished Egypt had a flat kid who would help out like that in a museum. A kid like that could come in handy, he said. He hung a bulletin board over my bed hoping that something might happen, but my mother made him take it down again."

"That's good," Stanley said. "Being flat is more trouble than some people imagine it to be."

Walk Like an Egyptian

Stanley found being out in the sunshine very pleasant after being cooped up in a dark envelope for so long. "Is it always this warm and sunny in Egypt?" he asked.

"It's not always this warm," Amisi answered, "but, yes, it's usually sunny. It doesn't rain often here, but when it does, we can get downpours." She pointed to a beautiful river in the distance, fringed with palm trees. "Sometimes the Nile floods. And in the spring we can get sandstorms."

Amisi was a very good guide. She pointed out mosques and gardens and historical sites. They stopped at a stall where she treated Stanley to some Egyptian food—falafel, kebobs, and dates. They ate as they walked, and Stanley found it all very tasty indeed.

"Well, here we are." Amisi nodded across the street to a narrow alleyway crowded with booths. "That's the antiquities bazaar you were addressed to." She turned and pointed to a sign above them: National Historical

Museum. "And here's where my father works. Would you like to come in? He'd be so thrilled to meet you."

Stanley wanted to get right to work on the archaeological adventure, but he knew being polite and friendly always paid off. "Lead the way," he said.

Amisi laughed as they stepped inside. "See those hieroglyphs? *They'll* lead the way."

Stanley admired the black images on the wall.

"Hieroglyphs were the writing system of pictures used by the ancient Egyptians. The people and animals were always drawn sideways, which told which direction to read them. My father had these painted to point the way to his office," Amisi explained.

As they walked through the rooms in the museum, Stanley saw many amazing things: golden masks and statues, silver and bronze coins, turquoise and ivory jewelry, beautifully decorated urns and pots. "Your country is full of treasures," he marveled.

"Yes," Amisi agreed. "But we're losing them. Criminals are looting the pyramids and then exporting the artifacts. My father says they are even worse than sneak thieves! Well, here we are."

They entered the office marked CURATOR. Inside, a tall, smiling man came over and hugged Amisi.

"Father, this is Stanley Lambchop," she said.

"Stanley Lambchop," Amisi's father repeated, scratching his head. "Hmm ... now where have I heard that name before?"

"Your pen pal's letter?" Amisi reminded him.

He slapped his head. "Holy sarcophagus! The sneak thieves hero?" He stood back and eyed Stanley up and down. "Yes, just as old Darty described you: flat as a pancake. What a thing! That bulletin board . . . it was hanging over your bed, is that the story? About how far off the floor?"

"Father," Amisi said, "remember, Mother strictly forbade you trying to flatten me."

"Right. Of course. Now, what brings you to our country, Stanley?"

Stanley explained about the request to help with an important archaeological expedition.

"Very interesting," said Amisi's

father. "Now, that bulletin board. Exactly how heavy was it . . . do you recall?"

"Father!"

"Of course, I know, I know. It's just that . . . so simple really . . . what a help to the Famous Museum. Really, Stanley, when Old Darty explained what you did, how brave you were . . ."

Stanley blushed. He really hadn't done much more than hang inside a picture frame and then yell for the police when the sneak thieves sneaked in. He didn't tell Amisi and her father this, but what had taken the most courage, actually, was wearing a dress in the painting.

"May I give you a personal tour of our museum?" asked Amisi's father. "It would be an honor."

"I'm sure I would enjoy that," Stanley said. "But the letter said the situation was urgent. I think it's time I got to work." He said good-bye to Amisi and her father and left the museum.

The Mission

The bazaar was colorful with over-
flowing displays and noisy with the
cheerful shouts of buyers and sellers.
Booths were piled with antiquities:
woven rugs and embroidered cloths,
ancient pottery and plates, brass
lamps, gold jewelry, silver brushes
and combs, decorated tablets and
scrolls. Everywhere, Stanley smelled

incense and perfume and spices. Donkeys brayed and carts jostled the crowds. Now and then, Stanley had to turn sideways to get through without bumping into anything.

"Sometimes," he reminded himself, "sometimes being flat makes me feel lucky."

"But mostly," he reminded himself back, "mostly being flat just makes me feel . . . flat."

He couldn't help wondering which way he would feel at the end of his adventure. If he ever *had* an adventure! How would he know he was at the right place? How would he find Sir Abu Shenti Hawara IV?

"Pssst . . . Flatly! You Flatly Porkchop?"

Before Stanley could correct whomever was there, an arm shot out and dragged him behind a hanging rug. "Come with me," said a man in a dark

uniform. "Sir's been waiting for you."
The man pulled Stanley through the
back alleys of the bazaar until they
came to a fenced-off tent surrounded
by more uniformed men. Inside, even
more guards nodded at Stanley and the

man and stepped aside.

Inside the tent was dark, with clouds of smoke rising from oil lamps and pots of incense. After a moment, Stanley made out a bearded man in a red robe seated on a gold embroidered cushion. Sir Abu Shenti Hawara IV clapped his hands and motioned for Stanley to approach, and then he nodded to a guard. "Turn him sideways," he ordered, pointing (very rudely, Stanley thought) to Stanley. "Measure him."

Stanley knew it was important to be polite, even when faced with rudeness. "I'm Stanley Lambchop, from America," he introduced himself. "I'm very pleased to meet you, and I hope—"

"You're not likely to pop out round in the middle of things, are you?" Sir Hawara interrupted. "This flatness isn't just a party trick, right?"

Stanley sighed. "Not so far."

The guard had finished the measuring. "One half inch thick," he reported.

"Good then," Sir Hawara said. "Let's get started. I've been waiting a long time for this." He clapped his hands again, and half a dozen guards sprang to his side. Several of them spread maps and photographs on the ground, while another lit his pipe.

"You smoke, Lambchop?" Sir Hawara asked.

Stanley shook his head no, wondering what his parents might say about this.

"Too flat, I suppose," Sir Hawara mused. He shook his head, and then tapped his pipe on the map in front of him. "This here is the great pyramid of Khufufull, sealed for more than four thousand years. It is believed that at the center, inside the pharaoh's tomb, are the priceless Giant Scrolls of Papyrus."

Stanley waved away some smoke. "And you're going to go in and find them?"

"Wrong," answered Sir Hawara. "*You're* going to go in and find them. That's why I've brought you here."

"But I don't know anything about—" Stanley began.

Sir Hawara ignored him. "According

to ancient lore, King Khufufull locked his tomb from the inside to protect it from grave robbers."

At the words *grave robbers*, Stanley shivered and broke into goose disks. (Since his encounter with the bulletin board, Stanley's goose bumps now came up as flat as the rest of him, more like tiny disks than bumps. "Nothing to be alarmed about," Doctor Dan had assured his parents when they'd noticed this. "Perfectly normal in these cases. I've been expecting it.")

"Also," Sir Hawara continued, "he had dozens of trick passageways built, leading nowhere. However, he did leave one way out: a passageway three inches wide—just wide enough for his soul to escape." He pointed his pipe at Stanley. "That's where you come in. I've found the entrance to that passageway. You're going to enter the tomb, find out if the scrolls are really there, and then unlock the tomb from inside. Got it?"

Stanley nodded.

"Good." Sir Hawara rose from his cushion and clapped his hands one more time. "Saddle up a camel for our flat friend," he ordered a guard. Then he turned to Stanley. "One hump or two?"

Stanley stared at him.

"That's a joke, Lambchop," Hawara said. "We only have one-humped camels here in Egypt."

In the Tomb

Stanley found that no matter how many humps a camel may have, riding one was no joking matter. The camel lurched. Stanley slipped. The camel bumped. Stanley slid. He finally solved the problem by folding himself over its hump like a blanket.

At last the caravan came to a stop. Stanley fell to the ground and looked

up. And up. Somehow, pyramids had always looked a bit smaller in pictures.

Sir Hawara brought Stanley around to the back, and then lit a torch and handed it to him. He pointed to a space just a few inches wide between two enormous stone blocks. "Remember, find the scrolls, and then unlock the tomb. No dillydallying."

Stanley stared at the dark slot between the stones. He didn't think it looked like a place he would want to be dillydallying. He didn't think it looked like a place he would want to do *anything* in, in fact. But he reminded himself that this was an important archaeological expedition, and a promise

was a promise. He took a deep breath and wedged himself into the passageway.

Three inches is not very much room to get around in. Stanley had to half wriggle and half slide as he took little sideways hops, just to inch along slowly. After many twists and turns in the deepest darkness, he heard a leathery flapping. He felt a rush of wind, as if from a great many wings. He held up his torch and then out of the gloom . . .

Bats! Hundreds of them! Thousands, perhaps! Stanley had disturbed a whole colony of bats, and they were coming right for him!

He felt himself break into a cold sweat and a new set of goose disks. As the bats approached, Stanley leaped up and pressed himself against the stone wall.

And he stuck there!

The goose disks on his arms and legs, in combination with the cold sweat, had become little suction cups! Stanley hung perfectly still, pressed tight to the pyramid wall like a starfish, until the entire flock of bats had passed by. Then, as his fear subsided, the little goose disk suction cups let go one by one—*thwop, thwop, thwop*—and he slipped gently to the ground again.

Stanley was badly shaken. But he knew he must go on. He took one sideways step, and then another and another. Just as he was beginning to give up hope of ever finding the tomb, the passageway opened up into an arched entryway.

Stanley held up his torch and gasped. He had been in several extremely fancy elevators before, so he was no stranger to beautiful places. But this was something else indeed!

Bejeweled carvings of dogs and snakes guarded the entryway. Gilded urns lined the walls. In the center of the room sat a large casket made of

gold. And on top of that lay a life-sized alabaster statue of King Khufufull!

There was no doubt about it—Stanley had discovered the tomb of the great pharaoh. And flanking the coffin, on golden pedestals, were two enormous scrolls.

He had done it! He had found the priceless Giant Scrolls of Papyrus!

Now to find the secret exit!

Stanley stepped into the tomb and began to search. The walls were covered with hieroglyphs and beautiful painted scenes. But there was no door! The only thing that seemed out of place was a large button at the far end of the tomb. The button seemed, strangely, to call to him. As if it were saying, *Press me!*

Stanley did. A panel swung open to reveal a full-sized passageway!

Stanley stepped out to explore and held up his torch. Surely this was the passageway Sir Hawara had talked about—the one the burial party must have used. But the passageway split just ahead, and from there, Stanley could see that each branch split again. How would he know which way to go to get out?

And then he noticed something: At each intersection, a life-sized hieroglyph was painted on the wall. What if . . . what if they were painted facing a certain way to give directions, like the ones in the National Museum . . . ?

A Bad Surprise

Stanley closed the tomb's door behind him and set off, following the hieroglyphs at every branch. Before long, he came to another button on the wall, just like the one in the tomb. He pressed it, and once again, a large panel—a huge block of stone—swung open. Stanley stepped outside into the fresh air.

Sir Hawara and his guards came rushing over when they saw Stanley. "Well?" Sir Hawara demanded, hopping on one foot and then the other. "The scrolls?"

"I found them," Stanley told him. Suddenly he felt quite proud: He had located the priceless Giant Scrolls of Papyrus! And now he was safely outside, in the warm sunshine! It had all been worth it. "And I found the passageway out. There are lots of branches in the passageway, but all you have to do is follow the black hieroglyphs to get out . . ."

"Excellent!" Sir Hawara rubbed his hands together. "I must get the crew ready. Meet me back here in the morning . . . at daybreak we take the scrolls!" He climbed onto his camel and rode away, leaving Stanley bewildered.

Just then he felt a tug at his shirt. He turned to find Amisi there, glaring at him.

"*That's* who you've been working with? That's the worst looter of Egyptian treasures in the country! My father and I have been trying to catch him red-handed for years. I guess I was wrong about you." And she stomped off.

47

Stanley didn't know what to think. He climbed back onto his camel and followed Sir Hawara's party back to the bazaar. He was going to find out just what was going on.

Back at Sir Hawara's headquarters, henchmen were everywhere. Stanley eased himself into the shadows and sneaked around to the back. He lifted the tent flap and peeked inside. It was even darker and smokier than before. Stanley took a deep breath of nice, fresh outside air. Then, using the limberness he had developed by slipping under his bedroom door at home, Stanley slipped under the flap.

Sir Hawara was on his cushion, talking in a low voice. Cautiously, Stanley crept closer so he could hear.

"What's that? In the shadows?" A guard jumped up, pointing toward Stanley!

There was no place to hide! Stanley plastered himself against a large container standing upright behind him and froze.

"It's nothing," said Sir Hawara, clapping his hands for silence. "Just the sarcophagus. It's a very realistic painting on the cover . . . quite a find. Now, pay attention to my plans!"

Stanley held himself perfectly still and listened keenly.

"Tomorrow, we send the flat boy into the tomb to unlock it for us. We take the scrolls and pack them onto a plane I will have waiting. We'll be out of there before anyone is the wiser. Those scrolls will fetch a fortune! I'll be rich, rich, rich! And the beauty of it all is that no one will ever know they existed!"

So Amisi was right! They were looters, who were sneakier than the worst sneak thieves, and Stanley was helping them steal one of Egypt's greatest treasures!

Stanley peeled himself off the sarcophagus quietly and slid back under the tent. Then he made his way to the National Historical Museum and climbed the steps. The least he could do was admit to Amisi and her father what he had done.

The entryway was crowded with tourists. Immediately Stanley found himself squashed in the center of a particularly careless group. After a moment, through a tangle of arms and cameras, he saw Amisi and her father come in. They passed right by him.

"What about a very *light* bulletin board?" he heard Amisi's father say. "What about . . . a *map*?"

"I don't think so, Father," Amisi replied. "Besides, I think that bulletin board flattened his brains! Wait until I tell you what I just found out!"

Stanley worked himself free from the crowd and hurried after Amisi and her father. He caught up with them at the curator's office and called out. Amisi turned and frowned at him. Then she slammed the door shut.

Somehow, Stanley felt . . . even flatter than before. As flat as the hieroglyph painted on the wall beside him.

And then he had an idea.

An idea that just might work . . .

Stanley ran to the main desk and scribbled a note. "Please give this to the curator," he said. "It's urgent. Thank you very much." Then he went back to the antiquities bazaar, planning his plan.

The sky was growing dark. Stanley let himself into the camels' pen, and there he made a bed for himself by placing a stack of saddle blankets on a mound of straw and then layering himself into the stack. He closed his eyes, remembering that his parents insisted he and Arthur get a good night's sleep every evening.

Suddenly, Stanley missed his family

very much. He wondered what they had been doing while he'd been gone . . . playing Monopoly? Looking at pictures of their last family vacation to Mount Rushmore? Without him? Stanley's stomach grumbled with hunger. What had his family had for dinner that night? Meatloaf and mashed potatoes, his favorite? With apple crisp for dessert, maybe?

Beside him, a camel grunted and snorted. If he were at home, Arthur would be sleeping in the bed next to him right now. Arthur sometimes grunted and snorted in his sleep, too, but Arthur smelled better than a camel, thought Stanley fondly, as he fell asleep.

Sneaky Plans

The next morning, Stanley awoke to more hand clapping—Sir Hawara was gathering his crew outside the camels' pen. Stanley lay between his blankets thinking he had had just about enough of all that hand clapping. He wondered why someone hadn't told Sir Hawara how rude it was. As Stanley lay there thinking, he wasn't paying attention.

He didn't notice that one of Sir Hawara's henchmen had come into the pen.

The man grabbed the stack of blankets Stanley was lying in and started piling them on the camels. And before Stanley could scramble out, the guard threw a saddle over the blankets and helped Sir Hawara onto it!

And so just as the sun was rising, Sir Hawara and a large group of his men took off for the pyramid of Khufufull— with Stanley along for the ride. If I hadn't been flattened already, Stanley thought, this would do the trick.

As they rode along, Sir Hawara continued to discuss his sneaky plan with his men. With each thing he overheard, Stanley felt worse. "We'll take everything, not just the scrolls!" "We'll pick that tomb clean as a lambchop bone!"

"Speaking of Lambchop bones, what about the flat boy?" Stanley heard someone ask. "He knows about the scrolls. What if he tells?"

"Don't worry about him," Sir Hawara answered. "Once he's unlocked the tomb, we don't need him anymore. We'll just seal him up in there. He can rot in that tomb for eternity with the mummies, and no one will ever know!"

Locked inside a tomb with the mummies to rot for eternity! How he would miss his family! How he would miss his friends at school—even the mean ones like Emma Weeks. Stanley hoped that Amisi's father had gotten his note. . . .

The caravan stopped at the base of the pyramid, and everyone hurried off.

Stanley worked his way out from under the blankets and followed them around to the back of the pyramid.

"Oh, there you are," Sir Hawara said, handing him a torch. "Now, just like last time: open the door from inside for us. Got it?"

Stanley nodded, took the torch, and squeezed himself into the narrow slot. He worked his way along the passageway as quickly as he could, and reentered the tomb. Inside, he stopped at the base of the pharaoh's coffin.

"Try not to worry," he said out loud. "If my plan goes well, they won't be gone for long." Stanley felt a little silly talking to a statue. But in the gloom, it almost looked as if the statue were smiling back at him.

Stanley pressed the button again, unlocking the tomb. And there, waiting in the main passageway, were Sir Hawara and his men, laden with carts and boxes.

Stanley put on his biggest smile as the crew rushed in. "Just remember . . . follow the hieroglyphs to get out. . . ."

The Hieroglyph

Sir Hawara's crew rushed into the pharaoh's tomb, nearly knocking Stanley over in its excitement.

From the passageway, Stanley could hear them exclaim over the treasures. Sir Hawara ordered them to start stripping the tomb: "If it's gold, take all you can hold!" he chortled. "Take everything you can carry! This guy's been dead for four thousand years . . . he won't miss anything! Follow the hieroglyphs and start loading the plane!"

It was time! Stanley extinguished his torch and covered himself all over with the soot. He whispered Sir Hawara's chilling words to himself, "We'll just leave him to rot with the mummies for eternity!" and felt himself break out into goose disks. He felt a cold sweat grow over them. And then he leaped up to the wall and froze there, stuck.

Sir Hawara's crew ran out of the tomb, loaded with treasures. Sir Hawara shone his flashlight along the walls of the passageway. His beam fell upon Stanley. "There's one!" he called. "Funny-looking thing, but it's just like the flat kid said—it's pointing the way. Come on!" He and his men rushed off.

In the wrong direction!

Stanley slipped down from the wall and made his way to the exit. As he stepped outside, he was delighted to see Amisi and her father waiting.

"We've brought the police, just as you asked," Amisi said. "But what's this all about?"

"Go on in," Stanley directed the police officers. "I think you'll find this pyramid is loaded with looting looters . . . loaded with loot!"

And that is exactly what they did find. After a few moments, the officers began to come out of the pyramid with Sir Hawara and his henchmen and the stolen artifacts.

"Caught red-handed at last!" Amisi and her father cried.

Stanley was especially happy to see Sir Hawara in handcuffs. . . . There would be no more hand clapping from him for a while!

Soon there was a big crowd around Stanley. "So smart! So brave! So flat!" people marveled when they found out the story. In the middle of the commotion, Amisi gave Stanley a hug. "I was wrong when I said I was wrong about you!" she said.

Stanley felt himself blush bright red. He wondered how he hadn't noticed it before: Amisi was very pretty.

Amisi's father came over and took a picture of the two of them with his instant camera. He gave the picture to

Stanley. "So you'll always remember your visit."

Then he shook Stanley's hand. "You've captured Egypt's worst looter and saved the priceless Giant Scrolls of Papyrus. Egypt's debt to you is enormous . . . how can we ever repay you? Say the word . . . whatever reward you'd like is yours."

Before Stanley could answer, the little celebration was disturbed by a group of tourists. They were laughing and pointing at Stanley's camel. "Look at the shape of that animal, Marge!" cried one man. "Absolutely ridiculous!"

Stanley knew too well how it felt to

be poked fun of because of one's shape. "Hey!" he called back, patting his camel. "We don't get to choose what we look like!"

Stanley could almost hear his mother's voice. "Hay is for horses, not people," she would remind him if she were here now. She was always one for proper language. Or, if she really were here in Egypt, she would probably say, "Hay is for camels." She was also always one to appreciate her surroundings.

Suddenly, Stanley missed his family again, even more than the night before. "Could you please just mail me back to America?" he asked.

"Certainly," Amisi's father replied. "Let's go inside and get you wrapped up now."

The words made Stanley remember something. "Just one more thing," he said. And then he asked Amisi and her father for a favor.

A Package for Arthur

Back at the Lambchop residence, George Lambchop arrived home from work early. "The office is being repainted," he explained to his wife. "Just as well. I wasn't getting much done. I keep wondering how Stanley's doing." He picked up the mail in the hall. "Say, Harriet!" he cried. "There's a large package here from Egypt! Do you think . . . ?"

"Yes, I know," Mrs. Lambchop said. "For a moment I was so excited. I thought our dear boy was back. But it's addressed to Arthur, not to us. I think Stanley has only sent a souvenir home early."

"I imagine you're right," Mr. Lambchop said, disappointed. "Besides, the package is just lying there quietly. That couldn't be Stanley!"

Just then, Arthur came home from school. Mr. Lambchop noticed he looked very glum indeed. "How about a game of Monopoly?" Mr. Lambchop offered. "Or a walk in the park to watch the sailboats?"

Arthur shook his head. "It wouldn't

be the same without Stanley here. Nothing's the same without Stanley here." He sighed.

"Well, this might cheer you up." Mr. Lambchop handed Arthur the package.

He and Mrs. Lambchop watched as their son opened it.

All three of them cried out in shock as a mummy sprang from the package! The mummy began reeling stiff-legged around the living room. Mrs. Lambchop almost fainted. Mr. Lambchop prepared himself to protect whomever might need protecting.

Arthur stared with his mouth hanging open. And then he started to

laugh. "This mummy is a little . . .
flat!"

Mr. and Mrs. Lambchop stepped closer to look for themselves. It was true! Even under all the wrappings, it was clear there was something oddly shaped about this mummy . . .

"Start unwrapping at once!" called Mr. Lambchop.

And so they did. Finally, after unwinding what seemed like miles of linen strips, there stood their own dear boy, Stanley!

What a surprise! There was great rejoicing and many hearty congratulations on Stanley's clever trick. Everyone talked at once. "We'll remember *that* for a long time!" "Ho, ho! And to think you were right under our noses all afternoon!" "How did you ever manage to stay so still?"

Then Mrs. Lambchop remembered she had dinner cooking. "Come to the table while it's still hot, please."

Over meatloaf and mashed potatoes (being careful not to talk with his mouth full), Stanley told about his adventure. At the part about Sir Hawara's plan to leave Stanley in the tomb, Mrs. Lambchop turned quite pale. She held her husband's hand for strength. But otherwise, everyone was quite delighted with the story. Many, many times, they exclaimed about how clever and how brave Stanley had been.

After the apple crisp was finished—seconds all around—Mrs. Lambchop decided the family had had enough excitement for one day. "Time for bed."

Stanley was very happy to see his old bedroom, with his spaceship lamp and his striped pajamas neatly folded on top of his soft pillow, just as he had left it. "It's good to be back," he told Arthur. Then he remembered the photograph Amisi's father had taken. He pinned it up on his bulletin board.

"That's Amisi," Stanley told his brother. "What do you think of her?"

"I think . . ." Arthur looked at the

photograph, puzzled. "I think she's a *girl*."

Stanley got into bed and turned out the light. "That's what I think, too, Arthur," he said. He smiled in the dark.

THE END

WHAT YOU NEED TO KNOW TO BE AN EGYPTOLOGIST

Egypt is in Africa, and its capitol, Cairo, is the biggest city on the whole continent.

The Nile river, which runs through Egypt, might be the longest river in the world. (It depends how you measure—some people think the Amazon is a little longer!)

The Great Pyramid of Giza is the only one of the Seven Wonders of the Ancient World that is still standing. It's built from more than two million blocks that each weigh as much as a pickup truck.

Ancient Egyptian hieroglyphic
writing includes about 800 symbols—
the English alphabet has only 26!

Ancient Egyptians mummified important
people after they died by wrapping them
in strips of cloth. The oldest known
mummy is more than 5,000 years old!

Much of Egypt is covered by
the Sahara desert, which is the
biggest sandy desert on earth.

JEFF BROWN created the beloved character of Flat Stanley as a bedtime story for his two sons. He has written other outrageous books about the Lambchop family, including FLAT STANLEY, STANLEY AND THE MAGIC LAMP, INVISIBLE STANLEY, STANLEY'S CHRISTMAS ADVENTURE, STANLEY IN SPACE, and STANLEY, FLAT AGAIN! You can learn more about Jeff Brown and Flat Stanley at www.flatstanleybooks.com.

SARA PENNYPACKER is an award-winning writer whose books for children include the endearing CLEMENTINE. She lives in Cape Cod, Massachusetts.

MACKY PAMINTUAN is an accomplished illustrator. He lives in San Diego, California, with his wife and dog.